KU-274-603

CONTENTS

SECRETS OF THE LIBRARY OF DOOM

THE BOOK THAT ATE ME

BY MICHAEL DAHL
ILLUSTRATED BY PATRICIO CLAREY

Raintree is an imprint of Capstone Global Library Limited, a company
incorporated in England and Wales having its registered office at 264
Banbury Road, Oxford, OX2 7DY – Registered company number: 6695582

www.raintree.co.uk
myorders@raintree.co.uk

Designed by Hilary Wacholz
Original illustrations © Capstone Global Library Limited 2022
Originated by Capstone Global Library Ltd
Printed and bound in India

978 1 3982 1358 6

British Library Cataloguing in Publication Data
A full catalogue record for this book is available from the British Library.

The Library of Doom is a hidden fortress.
It holds the world's largest collection
of strange and dangerous books.

Behold the Librarian. He defends the Library – and
the world – from super-villains, clever thieves
and fierce monsters. Many of his adventures
have remained secret. Now they can be told.

SECRET #3
SOME BOOKS GRAB YOU . . .
AND NEVER LET GO.

Chapter One

TRUE STORY

The story you are about to read is **TRUE**.

I'm a kid who didn't like reading before all this stuff happened.

Before I was **EATEN** by a book.

My story **STARTS** one night at the town library.

I have to write a school report on wild animals. So I'm looking at all the boring animal books.

Then I hear a noise.

GRRRRRRRRRRRRGGGGG

I turn around. All I see is a STRANGE
book sitting on the shelf by itself.

I pick it up. The cover feels **WARM**.

It's called *The Book of Beasts*.

Chapter Two

THE BOOK OF BEASTS

The library is about to **CLOSE**. I hurry to take out the book.

The man at the front desk gives me a funny look.

"This book isn't ours," he says. "Maybe someone forgot and left it **BEHIND**."

That's weird, I think. *But I need this book for my report. There is no time to look for another one.*

So I **SHOVE** it into my backpack.

I **RUSH** outside the library and down the stone steps.

Under the trees are some benches. I put my backpack on a bench and sit down.

Okay, let's have a good look at this book, I think. Hey! The book is **MISSING!**

Chapter Three

GROWL

Where did the book go?

GRRRRRRRRRRRRRRGGGGG

That sound again. It's coming from under the bench.

I look down and see *The Book of Beasts* lying open.

But it doesn't have paper inside. It has rows of **SHARP** teeth!

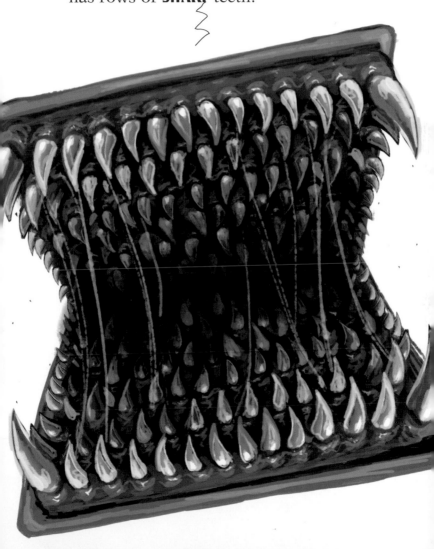

I **SCREAM** and jump up on the bench.
Too late!

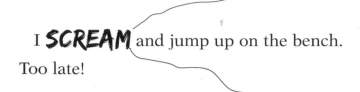

The book grabs my left foot in its jaws.
I try to SHAKE it off.

The book quickly swallows all
of my leg below the knee.

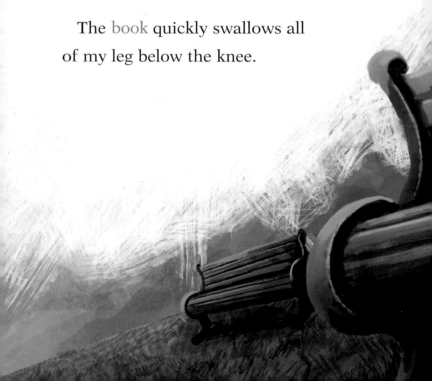

This is **IMPOSSIBLE!** I think. *Where is my leg going?*

My leg doesn't hurt. I can still feel it, even though it's inside the book.

I have to get help. I jump off the bench using my other leg.

But the **JAWS** won't let go.

I lose my balance and **FALL** on the grass.

GRRRRRRR!

The book is in my face! Then I am
surrounded by DARKNESS.

I am inside the book.

Chapter Four

GUTS

Suddenly I **BUMP** into something.

"Look out!" shouts a voice.

Light from a phone BLINKS on. I can see at least ten other people in the dark.

"What's going on?" I ask.

"We're **TRAPPED** in the book's stomach," says a scruffy looking kid.

The stomach looks like a small CAVE.

The walls and floor are made of paper. They're **COVERED** with letters and words.

"How long have you all been in here?"
I ask.

The people all **SHRUG**. "Two days?"
says one person.

"Three?" says another.

"Haven't you tried to get **OUT**?" I ask.

"There isn't a way out," says the scruffy kid. "We're **DEAD** meat."

"Well, I'm not going to sit around and wait for help," I say.

I reach into my pocket. I PULL out a pen.

By the LIGHT of several phones, I examine the walls. I see a big letter O.

I grip my pen. Then I **JAB** it right into the middle of the O.

OOOOOOOOHHHHHHHH!

The stomach rocks back and forth.

Everyone is **THROWN** to the floor.

"Stop!" yells a girl. "You're going to get us all killed!"

"Are you kidding?" I say. "We're already in a stomach. I don't want to end lower down!"

I POKE at the stomach again. This time at an E.

EEEEEEEEEEEEEEE!

Chapter Five

THE GUY

The book is **SHAKING** hard now.

People inside the stomach are **FALLING** and tumbling.

I poke at the wall, again and again. The paper is really thick.

But finally my pen makes a **HOLE**.

A beam of LIGHT gleams through the opening.

No, it's not a beam. It's a pair of scissors! The scissors are **MASSIVE**.

Holding on to the scissors is a guy in a long coat and dark glasses.

"Stand back," he says.

His scissors **CUT** a larger hole into the papery wall.

The girl stares at the guy in the glasses. "The legends are true!" she says. "You're the LIBRARIAN."

The Librarian? I think. *Who is he?*

"Quickly!" the guy **SHOUTS**. "Grab my hand!"

He helps each of us through the hole in the wall.

We **SQUEEZE** through, one by one.

I'm last. Once I get outside, everyone else is already gone.

The cool **AIR** feels good.

The guy looks at me and says, "You're really sharp."

"So are those scissors," I say.

Then, the guy does something really **WEIRD**. He hands me his scissors!

They look like **NORMAL** ones now.

"You might need these," he says.
"In case of emergencies."

The guy **POINTS** behind me.

"That should be harmless now," he says.
"But I'd like you to keep an eye on it."

The Book of Beasts is lying on the
ground.

I pick up the book. When I turn back, the guy is gone.

That's my story. It **ALL** happened. Really.

Since that **NIGHT**, things have been different.

I'm not just an average kid anymore.

Yeah, I read books now. But I also **HUNT** books.

I've decided I'm going to be the NEXT Librarian.

GLOSSARY

beast wild animal, especially one that is large, dangerous or unusual

emergency event that needs to be dealt with straight away

examine look at closely

gleam shine brightly

jab poke quickly or suddenly

legend old story that may or may not be based on true events or real people

massive very large and heavy

scruffy dirty and messy looking

sharp having a cutting edge or point; being very smart and clever

shrug lift one's shoulders as if to say you don't know or don't care

surround be on all sides of something

TALK ABOUT IT

1. Were you surprised that *The Book of Beasts* eats people? Look back through the story. Find at least two clues that hint the book is not normal.

2. This story is told by the boy. What do you think of this choice? How would the story be different if it was told from the Librarian's point of view?

WRITE ABOUT IT

1. Do you agree with the boy's decision to poke the book's stomach? Or do you think his plan was too risky? Write a paragraph arguing for your choice.

2. Write about the boy's next adventure. What strange book does he hunt down next? How does he defeat it?

ABOUT THE AUTHOR

Michael Dahl is an award-winning author of more than 200 books for young people. He especially likes to write scary or weird fiction. His latest series are the sci-fi adventure Escape from Planet Alcatraz and School Bus of Horrors. As a child, Michael spent lots of time in libraries. "The creepier, the better," he says. These days, besides writing, he likes travelling and hunting for the one, true door that leads to the Library of Doom.

ABOUT THE ILLUSTRATOR

Patricio Clarey was born in 1978 in Argentina. He graduated in fine arts from the Martín A. Malharro School of Visual Arts, specializing in illustration and graphic design. Patricio currently lives in Barcelona, Spain, where he works as a freelance graphic designer and illustrator. He has created several comics and graphic novels, and his work has been featured in books and other publications.